RUNNER AVAILABLE

RUNNER AVAILABLE

by

Michael Anthony White

VOX GEEKUS

The content within this book is of none other than 100% fiction. By no means is any said content to be taken as anything other than jovial nonsensicality and fantastical whimsy.

All information presented henceforth is to be regarded purely as imaginative rubbish scooped forth from the figurative cellars of the author's childish mind, representing nothing and/or no living beings in actual existence. No scenarios or situations are to be considered as legal advice, production direction, small business advisories, hygienic practice, or any possible semblance of instructional teaching whatsoever involving any human or non-human activity imaginable. The publisher and the author assume no responsibility for the actions of the reader.

To the maximum extent permitted by law, the publisher and the author disclaim any and all liability for errors, inaccuracies, omissions, or any other inconsistencies herein.

Copyright © 2024 Michael Anthony White
Cover art by Inorai

All rights reserved. No part of this book may be reproduced in any manner whatsoever without written permission except in the case of brief quotations embodied in critical articles and reviews.

First Printing, 2024

ISBN 979-8-9903738-1-5 (paperback)

Published by Vox Geekus

*To those who identify as geeks,
and those who do not...*

*To those who are Gen-X,
and those who are not...*

*To those who experienced
Saturday morning cartoons,
and those who did not...*

This is for you.

1

REBEL HQ MASTER LOG
5/13 6:07 p.m.

Our favourable efforts notwithstanding, the ImperiCorp organisation's megavirus continues to evolve at a threatening rate.

Vehicles, communication devices, and unsuspecting fixtures from vending machines to traffic signals are vulnerable to the reprogramming and utilisation for corporate surveillance, reacting with aggressive behaviour if provoked after infection.

With an insidious array of commandeered machines, ImperiCorp has thinned our offensive forces to three remaining agents: Jett, Nerva, and Lorik.

The last of the Runners.

Through the sacrifices of our fallen comrades, we have at last acquired the technology to develop an indispensable addition to our meagre arsenal: Panicsuits.

Monitoring the vitals and kinetics of those who wear them, these dark crimson garments transport the agent back to headquarters when the imminence of mortal trauma is detected.

The Runners continue to vigilantly refine their expertise by means of virtual simulations. Combining these drills with a regimen of optimal nutrition and rest, they patiently await a calling from our clandestine allies known only as The Fates, who inevitably summon our heroes to action once more with the use of Glimmer Rings.

Visible through the head-up display of Runners' bionic ocular implants, these azure beacons illuminate a strategically plotted route through which the ImperiCorp mainframe may be best infiltrated and neutralised.

Such a victory will in turn exterminate the megavirus and release the city from the digital chokehold that threatens to crush the trachea of the citizens' last hope for freedom.

2

NERVA'S LOG
5/13 6:09 p.m.

I'm here in my bunk awaiting my next chance to run and my pacing's been totally halted.

I just heard a voice ring out from a distant nowhere.

"...*need your help*..."

It faded in and out. Only that fragment.

Of *course* I'm spooked.

The young voice was female. Soft and kind.

And I'm currently the last female left in The Rebellion.

I know I'm not the first to hear strange voices... I've seen it mentioned in fallen Runners' disclosed logs. Sometimes they heard them when all alone in their bunk and other times when under fire in the field.

I've always chalked it up to them breaking under pressure.

I swear the voice *I* heard came right through my PA speaker but dispatch said nobody here at headquarters sent or received any transmissions like that.

They told me I was imagining things.

Has my mind been broken after just one run?

I... heard another voice earlier this week but couldn't make it out.

I'd mentioned it to Lorik and he said it could have been a traumatic response like maybe I was exhausted or in shock from my first run.

I later convinced myself it was just static.

This time the voice was crystal clear. It was faint but I know what I heard.

So distinct.

I don't know what I'm supposed to do about it.

We've paid so much for our progress and I need to keep my psyche in check now more than ever.

I'm still completely rattled. I mean *sure...* the Panicsuit saved my life during my first run but the experience was surreal and jarring. What if it fails to activate next time?

Maybe I need more training after all.

Maybe I've had too much.

Despite all my knowledge of computers and codes and how to crack them I have no clue where that voice came from.

But it was soft and kind.

Was it The Fates? *Another* ally reaching out to me?

...Was it really just in my head?

I'm hungry. I'm grabbing a Vita-pint and then putting all of this out of my mind. There's enough going on inside there and I can't deal with any distractions.

Besides... The Fates might not call on me again if Rebel Headquarters tips them off that I've lost it.

3

REBEL HQ MASTER LOG
5/13 6:10 p.m.

> Runner Available.

4

JETT'S LOG
5/13 6:15 p.m.

My nerves buzzed when I heard the gentle tone of the activated Glimmer Ring through the PA speaker, and as the light in my bunk illuminated, I grew a proud smirk, and stretched with anticipation.

The Fates had called me.

My extended time in training had boosted my confidence to the nth degree, and I was ready to serve ImperiCorp their eviction notice.

Donning a Panicsuit and quickly transporting to the surface, I grabbed a pulse orb from the cache and carefully secured it in my pack along with my plasma blade.

Peering through the Glimmer Ring, I took one look at that cursed building in the distance, that monstrosity built of ego and evil, feeling so resolute that on this day my own hands would mark its end.

Nerva and Lorik were the first Runners to test the Panicsuits, Lorik having two runs under his belt.

Nerva, being the most prominent of rebels at cracking code, shared her discovery with us upon her first Panicsuit return — a laughable and most cliché vulnerability within the design of the megavirus.

By analyzing a log salvaged from one of many drones effortlessly disabled by her own craft, it was learned that with a single well-placed pulse orb, destroying the mainframe held within the ImperiCorp skyscraper will instantly deactivate all infected machines.

Additionally, it will prompt all ImperiCorp drones to permanently delete their own logs, after which they become triggered to self-destruct.

A desperate measure, assumedly to prevent any opposition from stealing their technology.

No matter — we Runners plan on obliging that wish when we blow their precious corporate supercomputer into oblivion.

I am rambling; I need to focus detailing these logs with my activity.

After I took my first cautious step through the Glimmer Ring on the surface at Rebel Headquarters, it faded quickly from view. As expected, a successor appeared as a bold pixel on the map of my ocular HUD.

Eager as I was to reach that next checkpoint, I refused to permit haste to foil my strategy.

I would never best Lorik when it came to speed; a phaser blast was too quick for *me* to dodge, yet at this distance from ImperiCorp Headquarters, only their lower-class units, Phaserdrones, are found on patrol.

Becoming one with the shadows remains my specialty, and darkness is still darkness to humans and Phaserdrones alike.

Superdrones and other advanced models will be equipped with long-range thermal imaging and more, demanding that I exercise more complex tactics to evade them.

As was learned from our training, courses presented by the Glimmer Rings vary with each calling, presumably adjusted by members of The Fates to confound the drones alerted by prior Runners.

I admit I did not expect the distances between rings in the field to be as vast as they were — clearly a shortcoming of our training program.

Nevertheless, I saw this as an advantage; by nature, this provided more options in which I could practice my stealth maneuvers as I traversed the terrain.

By the time I restrained my excitement after stepping forth, dusk had already begun to caress the skyline.

The next Glimmer Ring was a quarter mile to the northeast. Ample trees and fields overgrown with browning weeds near the outskirts of our headquarters facilitated an effortless approach to the city's edge.

Picked up by my ocular radar among the faded foliage was little to be found other than scraps of metal that posed no threat, and they began to speckle the outer streets of the city more densely as I progressed toward the bold pixel.

Sunlight had nearly disappeared by the time I reached the first Phaserdrone, which proved equally as useless as the scraps encountered.

I found the range of its visual proximity sensor easily avoidable, as the machine floated along clumsily down the center of a side street remaining oblivious to my presence — even upon its swift impalement from my plasma blade.

It dropped like a deflated arena ball into my readied hands before I stashed it in an alley with ease.

The condition of the streets themselves was, undeniably, quite a sight. Faded strips of paint partnered alongside the square outlines marking occasional bits of reflective road studs from years past are a depressing scene in a *virtual* environment, and exponentially more so in person.

These glaring reminders of a formerly thriving metropolis linger everywhere.

Rarely do vehicles roam these roadways at dusk, and the few citizens I have spotted are shuffling wearily as they move about the sidewalks.

Even from the edge of this shallow, rancid alley in the dim of evening I can see the will to live fading from their exhausted eyelids with their every lethargic blink.

This is where I complete this first entry.
I will log my next upon arrival of the ring.

5

LORIK'S LOG
5/13 6:16 p.m.

I'm watchin' Jett's run on my ocular HUD and can't help shakin' my head.

Kid's got wicked skill, I'll give him that, but come on. He's gotta watch his pace.

I've always had to keep him in check during our drills. Guy's got enough confidence to make Ares blush. He hasn't learnt that stealth and speed are a recipe for a phaser blast to the midsection. They don't work together. Ya gotta pick one.

Speakin'a kids, I had a chat with Nerva after lunch today, poor thing. She's startin' to lose her cool and hear funny voices in her head, but it's nothin' a couple more runs can't fix.

She's just nervous.

I think she'll be good once she learns to trust the Panicsuits. Our former rebels fought with their lives to get this tech and get it right.

Yah, we'll be fine, and even better once those ImperiCorp trash are outta the picture.

She'll agree when we're all sittin' on a rooftop with a strong drink toastin' the end o' those clowns.

It'll work out. Long as she keeps those voices down.

6

JETT'S LOG
5/13 6:24 p.m.

When I arrived at the second Glimmer Ring, to my surprise — an unmarked rebel safe house waited nearby to welcome me with medical supplies, and a boost in morale.

This was appreciated, as my cover was nearly blown some blocks away from my arrival. I will be flaunting a small scar for the better part of a year to reminisce about the occasion.

A parked sedan with its engine smoothly idling had caught my ear when I was rounding the final cross street before my objective.

All seats were devoid of passengers, hazard lights blinking, tinted windows widely cracked.

That is a trap *defined.*

The megavirus is not sentient. No software is, nor will any ever be, regardless of how sophisticated.

Software upgrades require developers, and ImperiCorp spared no expense when it came to enhancing the capabilities of the megavirus.

Vehicles were an early target, easily infected through wireless audio signals. The virus's code would be downloaded to the vehicle's storage drive, eventually sabotaging the machine and causing random bursts of acceleration at the most detrimental opportunities.

Many innocent citizens were, in effect, successfully framed for reckless driving.

Even manslaughter.

Society caught on soon enough, and ImperiCorp learned from its mistake of invoking far too obvious of a phenomenon.

So they schooled themselves on playing dirtier, and made some "improvements."

An upgraded megavirus fully infiltrated vehicles' cameras and GPS. It targeted lone drivers visiting establishments with licenses to serve alcohol, surmising *that individual* would be a likely imbiber.

This element of the algorithm proved an accurate assumption.

Any payment methods the driver had saved to their vehicle's interface were trackable, so when a transaction including alcohol was detected at said place of business, the virus did its dirty work upon the driver's return:

Over-acceleration, under-acceleration, riding the brake, disabling headlights, and swerving.

In court, drivers with a recorded BAC of *any* level had a hard time pinning ImperiCorp as the guilty party.

Vehicles had become key weapons in ImperiCorp's arsenal, effective in draining the last of morale from the working class.

That was not enough. They had to outsmart us rebels.

Automation was ultimately implemented; the virus could eventually activate a parked car and operate it remotely. As idling vehicles are less conspicuous than those moving, they began to show up parked in half-empty lots and alongside curbs to draw less attention.

The population became paranoid of tinted or closed windows implying an empty driver's seat, and adopted the habit of rolling their windows down to prove their human presence — like medieval knights raising the visors of helmets to reveal their identities.

In response, ImperiCorp further raised the bar.

The act of flicking on hazard lights to indicate one's intent to quickly return to a vehicle had long been a common human behavior.

Citizens knew this.

So did ImperiCorp, and an upgraded virus adopted the behavior to draw less attention.

This was a lethal combination for earlier unsuspecting Runners to be plowed down by hell on wheels.

Over time, it became an obvious ambush to spot; there *were* no humans parking on curbs to run up to an ATM anymore. Most ATMs were either empty shells pilfered by criminals, or had become infected.

People were no longer quickly dashing into a convenience store. Any remaining retail operators did business by security window, which was far from expeditious; gone were the days of stepping inside brick and mortar to peruse goods and groceries.

To a Runner, an empty and idling vehicle parked on a curb with hazards on and windows down meant one thing and one thing only:

It was an infected death machine that for all intents and purposes now belonged to ImperiCorp.

I apologize — another tangent, stating the obvious.
I suppose it serves as catharsis.

Having spotted that red flag of a vehicle, I ascended a rugged downspout of the residential block on the opposite side of the street, carefully hopping and shimmying across the third story balconies.

No downtown residents were foolish enough to have neglected the drawing of blackout curtains, making it easy for me to avoid attention.

The attention of *sober* residents, as it turned out.

In the shadows of a middle balcony sat a pathetic youth no more than 15 years old, paranoid and twitching from high dosing.

He made it clear no visitors were welcome.

Seizing the closest flowerpot housing a packed volume of long-depleted soil, that angry child hurled it toward my head with impressive accuracy, while trembling and screaming obscenities through a strained larynx.

And then another.

By the time I scrambled to the next platform, the second pot that shattered upon it caught the attention of the hulking shirtless resident within the flat.

Whether he was convinced I was a burglar or a junkie was of no significance.

The man emerged from a sliding balcony door, joining in the obscene exclamations while swinging a charged club.

Preferring not to endure the embarrassment of explaining to headquarters that my Panicsuit's transport module had been initialized due to the repeated blows of a vigilante resident, I did the needful:

I leapt from the balcony down to the second story fire escape of the adjacent building, scampering in a frenzy across another before dropping and rolling onto the ground ten feet below.

My legs and torso were undamaged from my technique — that being said, I suffered a moderate gouge in my left hand from the rusty corner of a wrought iron rail.

What irked me most is that my Panicsuit's tolerance level dropped four points, putting it at 96%.

After shouting their final violent threats, both residents retreated to their quarters once losing their visuals on me as I returned to the darkness.

The pain throbbing from my hand was real, yet the company of a newly attracted friend demanded my full attention:

A Phaserdrone had been alerted, and it was sputtering my way.

Rather closely, at that.

As the furnishings of alleyways happen to be reliably basic, a dumpster was at the ready.

Phaserdrones however are not so basic.

For what they lack in visual capabilities, they make up for with their audio sensors. I could not risk diving into the garbage bin to hide without making a racket, so I snuck around it and crouched low.

After sweating bits of my soul for two minutes, the hovering drone lost interest and continued down its path, patrolling the remainder of the sidewalk.

Once able to proceed behind it, I did so with silence, dashing along the darkest walkways available to reach the Glimmer Ring.

With my blood circulating at a more than healthy rate, I arrived here at friendly shelter to be tended to by three fellow rebels.

I felt like a celebrity when they greeted me by my title.

"Runner! This way, please!"

The entrance is masterfully obscured. It is well-crafted of worn cinder blocks which blend into the dilapidated sidewall of an old public restroom, the original entrance door now unmarked and securely welded shut.

No more than 200 square feet, this hideout is accessible only by the covert portal from which I have been admitted, and a single grate in the tile floor.

The air inside is filtered and sterile.

Their supplies are few, yet sufficient: three oxygen masks, the aforementioned medical kits, rations including dried protein bars and Vita-pints, two portable comm-stations, and a small manual generator.

As the stationed rebels are not as extensively trained in survival as Runners, they utilize the sewers to travel between hideouts when inventory needs replenishing — which is seldom.

They have dressed my hand with professional care, yet my suit level still indicates a loss of 4%.

I plan on taking another moment's rest before making my way deeper into the city to reach my next objective, as it taunts my view with another bold pixel.

7

IMPERICORP HQ MASTER LOG
5/13 6:25 p.m.

    Phaserdrone unit #I34 reported a domestic disturbance during its patrol route in the southwestern quadrant.
    Mild damage to private landscaping accessories identified.
    Threat level: Nominal.

8

NERVA'S LOG
5/13 6:26 p.m.

Every part of me wants to break the rules to help Jett.

The Rebellion made it totally clear that we're only allowed access to disclosed archives from Runners... *no longer in service*... but it would be so easy to tap into Jett's logs.

For me anyway.

No. I would never do that... with only three of us Runners left our mutual trust is too sacred. These are my friends and The Rebellion is my family.

Every blink of Jett's marker on my map makes my insides bubble up with anxiety.

What if *his* suit fails? He's never used it before.

I wish The Fates could read my journals. Whoever they are.

I just want to help.

I want us to be okay.

9

JETT'S LOG
5/13 6:34 p.m.

    Another personal injury has been incurred, and my Panicsuit is now at 84%.

    Furthermore, in order to remain undetected, I inadvertently discharged my pulse orb shortly after leaving the safe house.

    As I advanced, deactivating two pairs of Phaserdrones proved simple enough, though disposing of the evidence posed more of a challenge.

    It seems the corporation has dispatched Class II Phaserdrones earlier than expected. Runners discovered partial development plans two months ago, however we had not expected ImperiCorp to have them operational so soon.

    It seems they have upped their game — these new models clearly possess more advanced scanning capabilities.

    One of the defeated Phaserdrones (sporting the signature mark of a plasma blade) that I had deposited into a dumpster was identified presumably by a Class II patrol.

    All units within a three-block radius were alerted to its presence:

One Superdrone, three standard Phaserdrones, and *presumably* one Class II unit.

Superdrones, with their crude humanoid skeletal likeness made of heavy clunking steel and phasers mounted on both shoulders are anything one would call subtle; I had plenty of time to confound its 30-yard line of sight by sprinting around the nearby corner of a decrepit industrial warehouse.

The most distant Phaserdrone echoed loudly as it floated down two blocks from the north, conspicuous as could be.

It was not a problem.

The two other standard units were rerouted from their nearby symmetrical patrols from the eastern blocks and had rendezvoused with one another upon being alerted to the location of my exposed kill. Per protocol, they were traveling in a pair down the center of the street. This made them easier to spot.

Again, *they* were not a problem.

The Class II would be the troublemaker to hurl a wrench into my gears.

A Class II's propulsion system contains no moving parts, allowing it to navigate a whisper-quiet, steady route. This more than makes up for its lack of visual range and can mean trouble for an unprepared Runner.

It surprised me as it zipped out from a lateral gutter from the side of the warehouse.

Hovering down from the rusty channel, it gracefully descended to three feet above ground level, and that is when I learned of its other specifications.

Like its predecessor, the Class II sports a short 15-foot optical range. The problem arose when I discovered that opposed to a frontal cone of vision, its sensors function omnidirectionally.

The Rebellion had failed to obtain this little piece of intel.

The machine's tiny phaser turret rotated with such increased speed compared to its inferiors, I almost thought for a moment that I saw the flash of its discharge.

After several exhalations from my distressed lungs, I realized I had instinctively readied the pulse orb from my pack and hurled it at the drone for a direct hit.

With a reticent burst of charged electromag powder, the drone succumbed to gravity, falling lifeless onto the tarmac.

Alas, the detonation had blown a fragment of the drone's outer casing into my torso, causing me — and my Panicsuit — to suffer a moderate hit.

Gathering the heavy remains of the drone, I retreated into the warehouse. Standing in shock from the speed of my own instincts, I swallowed repeatedly to stifle the vomit welling up in my esophagus.

Despite the evidence that my training was effective on a reflex scale, my judgment had been poor.

I now needed another pulse orb.

Undesirable as it was, I was forced to veer from my primary objective to reach the closest rebel cache on my map.

First, I had to escape that little platoon of death.

The echoing clunks of the Superdrone had come to a halt as it joined the other units at the dumpster down the block.

Whether or not they would discover more evidence of my handiwork and summon more backup to the area was of no consequence; I was already plotting my exit.

This required heading further northwest into the Gray District.

Our maps remain most outdated in this region, it being the previous home of an ImperiCorp research center.

A former Runner had successfully infiltrated the site and planted their pulse orb in the main generator room, where it failed to detonate due to a most untimely fault.

It was a dud.

Sorely regrettable, that incident convinced the corporation to migrate their complete facilities to that sinister skyscraper in the Central Zone, where they have bolstered their defenses exponentially.

We have since improved the pulse orb's design to a prevailing 100% success rate, and I intend to exhibit its efficacy once replenishing my inventory.

Superdrones loosely peppered the main streets of the Gray District amongst dense clusters of standard Phaserdrones, which meant opting to travel underground.

The inoperative sewer system in that zone had long dried up, and I wished I could say the same for the fetid stench.

That is a wish that was not granted.

Drones have no reason to enter the sewers outside of pursuing an identified Runner, so I traveled at a careful, quiet pace.

Stepping lightly through channels of waste is a task no rebel should endure.

I soon lost my bout versus the vomit bubble in my chest and ejected it from my sweating lips with a gag, squinting my eyes from the burn of the foul air around me.

As my vision blurred from the tears dripping from my bloodshot sclerae, it had become clear that I would need to quicken my pace and ascend from those noxious tunnels or face a battle of sickness none would envy.

Increasing my stride to a feeble jog to press through the slog, I angled around a final left turn and climbed to the top of the exit ladder — when I heard the clunking of metal above ground and froze.

The sounds of a Superdrone.

Fresh air was teasing mere inches above me at street level, and my fingers shook as I desperately cracked open the utility lid.

Cautiously swiveling my head to peek through a tactful sliver of the round street cover, my apprehensions were suddenly allayed upon identifying the source of the clamor.

It was no Superdrone — a citizen was trying their luck at breaking and entering, and not very successfully.

Sunken eyes sat atop a middle-aged woman's wiry frame as she slammed the rusty padlock of a shuttered cafe with a heavy tire iron, her mouth clinching in a toothy grimace on one side with every blow.

I slid open the hefty cover in full, violently shoving it across the surface of the sidewalk to announce my presence as the night air dried my irritated eyes.

There was not a hint of fear in the lady's gaze as she glanced briefly in my direction with worn teeth exposed, then returned to the rhythmic blows without missing a beat.

As she carried on with her business, I did so with mine.

My first instance of being nearly bested by a drone in the field had me mildly paranoid, so I climbed up a nearby fire escape with haste, deciding the rooftops would be my best friends to keep me company until I replaced the orb. Not a single drone patrols the rooftops of the Gray District.

There is an eerie beauty about the city at night when viewed from high elevation. The debris from long-term acts of vandalism on the streets below is obscured. Subtle reflections of stars upon unbroken windows of upper floors create a convincing mirage of a civilized, functional society in which one could thrive.

Those days have long gone — yet as I continue my trek, I am determined to see them again, in the daylight, on street level.

With some daring jumps I arrived at the edge of the final northwestern block, slid down six ladders and a gutter pipe, and sprinted across the vacant highway into the neighboring residential zone.

There, the marker on my map began to pulsate.

The hidden cache was 60 yards to the west, disguised as an empty bus stop shelter.

Having adopted a walking pace to avoid looking suspicious to the very occasional passerby, I discreetly approached the destination, and placed my left hand on the facade of a broken bus schedule display.

A nearby concrete slab slowly depressed and slid open to reveal the inventory, which was a welcomed sight.

I managed to rinse my eyes of the acidic sting from the sewers that rasped my tortured senses, as the cache of orbs was thoughtfully accompanied by first aid kits complete with ocular solution.

Indulging in that soothing fluid, it felt fantastic to blink with cleanly moistened eyelids once more — nevertheless I grew tired.

The temptation to grab more than one pulse orb was tantalizing. Even so, I recalled the hindrance their size inflicted upon my stealth movements during virtual drills, so a single orb was all I recovered.

The slab returned inaudibly to its tightly closed position upon my stepping away, and a long slow stretch of my back offered some rejuvenation before returning across the highway to re-enter the fray.

With a deep breath I stretched once more and picked up my gait, bounding to the rooftops with finesse.

I have since arrived back inside the decrepit warehouse, remaining unseen from the drones that scouted the northwestern streets.

I am sure this comfort will last only until the next Glimmer Ring, as it lies several blocks further east — adjacent to the Central Zone.

There, ImperiCorp's heavy turrets are inevitably to be expected.

Fortunate as I was to avoid any encounters since reaching the cache, pairs of Superdrones are strategically patrolling the corners of every other intersection below.

I am confident my precise location is unknown to them — though with the earlier stir I caused, I must presume ImperiCorp is unquestionably aware of my presence in the city.

10

IMPERICORP HQ MASTER LOG
5/13 6:35 p.m.

Class II unit #J42 reported Phaserdrone unit #I47 has been deactivated. Plasma blade evidence identified.

#J42 also reported Phaserdrone units #I11 and #I38 have failed to return status queries; considered deactivated.

Active Runner presumed within city limits.

Threat level: Moderate.

All drones notified.

11

NERVA'S LOG
5/13 6:36 p.m.

Something is happening to me...
But I don't think I'm losing it anymore.
I heard them again just now.
"don't give up...know...can do this."
It was a *different* voice. Clearer than the last and with such a caring and confident inflection.
It has to be The Fates trying to contact me.
I think they're trying to tell me I'm the one that's going to succeed in bringing down the megavirus...
To let me know I've got what it takes.
I have no idea how they're transmitting their messages. They must be using some sort of technology we don't understand yet.
Rebel Headquarters has told us so little about The Fates... I didn't feel before that we could fully trust them but now I feel it. Now I'm *certain* they're helping us.
I just wish I knew more about the who or where they came from...
Do they have a base of their own? How many members do they have?
Are they even human?

They've been so cryptic of their own identities they could be aliens or from the future for all we know.

Unless our leader is holding back intel?

I guess it doesn't matter. As long as they want to destroy ImperiCorp they're on our side.

Right?

My instincts have always told me that...

Wait. My bunk light flickered on right now.

What happened to Jett? ...Is he okay?!

He hasn't returned.

He... he *is* okay... he's still running! Unless my HUD is malfunctioning?

Oh my gosh... as I'm logging this Rebel Headquarters just confirmed through the PA.

I've been called and they've ordered my transport to the surface.

I've also been told my nanogloves have been upgraded.

Their maximum scan range has been increased by 25%.

That's massive!

This *is* happening.

I hope Jett's okay.

12

REBEL HQ MASTER LOG
5/13 6:37 p.m.

An additional calling from The Fates has been received during an active run.

Runner Available.

13

NERVA'S LOG
5/13 6:48 p.m.

It's as if everything I knew was wrong.

I don't hold The Rebellion to blame because we're all doing the best with the intel we've acquired but so much has happened in these first moments of my second run I feel both unprepared and enlightened.

After slipping back into my Panicsuit and making sure my nanogloves were strapped on tight I loaded up my belt pack with two pulse orbs.

At first I'd prepped my brain with the notion it would take some time to meet up with Jett.

So you can imagine my shock and relief that when I entered the first Glimmer Ring outside headquarters I was transported...

To his exact location.

I'd never heard of two Runners being called to the field at the same time so I didn't know what to think.

Let's just say my mind has been blown and in the best way.

Jett was startled to see me too but he looked like he was sure keeping his cool more than I was.

Then again he's used to playing things close to the belt.

"Well, now. Nice to see a friend."

I stared back impressed by his poker face.

"Jett! What... aren't you surprised I'm standing here?"

He raised an eyebrow at me and only a side-smile cracked open.

I never knew what to make of it when he smiled.

Sometimes he grinned as a way to hide when he was either confused or sizing people up. Other times it was sincere.

I could rarely tell the difference.

"Of course. Are you going to let me in on your little trick, or keep me in the dark?"

I grinned back.

"Well you've always said that *is* where you're the most comfortable."

I heard us both let out a nervous laugh before I realized it was just me.

I always thought I'd be alone during a live run and this was an odd feeling having a comrade by my side.

Odd but thankful.

Jett didn't seem to share my sentiment at first.

"We should split up."

"What? Why? We can help each other..."

"No doubt. Even so, I need to remain unseen if I am to be of any use to you — that is, unless you want all the glory for yourself."

He smiled again. This time with a wink and a real nod to let me know he was joking and I could finally tell he was just as happy as I was to have backup.

"How are we going to keep in touch? If we use comms in the field then ImperiCorp will triangulate our exact location in seconds. We're going to end up back in Rebel Headquarters to start all over again from the outskirts... if we even *get* called again."

He blew air out from his lips seeming irritated but it wasn't me he was angry at.

"They already know I am here."

"You? *You* blew cover already?"

He clinched his sculpted jaw and stared diagonally at the ground.

I could tell he was ashamed.

"The Class IIs have been deployed, Nerva. Here outside the Central Zone. One of them spotted me; they have omnidirectional visuals. I did not see that coming."

He turned toward me to reveal the Paniscuit tolerance indicator on his left sleeve.

Like we *really needed* this. I was already enough on edge after hearing those voices...

I trust Jett had no clue about it since I still hadn't told him. And I *know* Lorik would never have mentioned it to anyone.

But Jett had a plan as usual.

His map showed the next Glimmer Ring at the west side of the Central Zone at 33, 57.

Mine matched.

We decided to stay at least one block apart while traveling eastbound to meet up at a halfway point... 29, 44.

It wasn't much but at least we could share any intel we might dig up along the way.

He wished me luck before sprinting deeper into the northeastern half of the warehouse.

I blinked a couple times and he was gone...

It was time for *me* to show the corporation what I was made of so I stepped outside and held up my right hand to scan the environment as I slowly turned.

My new nanogloves were fancier alright. Their functions were quicker and I was provided with *way* more details than my last pair.

The scan covered more than half of the block to my southeast. It also added a red highlight to possible threats and pinned them to my map.

It detected one ATM... two abandoned vehicles... a fizzy drink vending machine... and one Superdrone marching down the middle of the avenue.

Across the street to the south was an old market next to a pharmacy. Both businesses were wedged between two parking structures.

Those kinds of places never stay open after dark. Their security windows are great for stopping burglaries and armed assaults but nobody gets paid enough to put up with harassment from the dope fiends when they come out at night.

Stealing food and drugs is all they care about when their stash runs dry and even though it takes an elephant to force open a security window it never stops them from trying.

They only give up and walk away when their fingers start bleeding at the tips.

Superdrones do *not* patrol alone this close to the Central Zone so I played it smart...

After crossing the road I bolted into the parking garage. I used the huge pillars inside as cover and would have plenty of room to fry the scanned Superdrone once it was far enough from any other units.

At that point it was 25 yards away walking east toward the next cross street.

A moment later I caught sight of another walking north into the middle of the same distant intersection.

It stopped and turned my direction as I instinctively crouched behind my hefty concrete cover... even though I was outside the limits of the Superdrones' basic visuals I didn't want to get caught if either of them initiated a long-range infrared scan.

I carefully peeked out around the corner of the large pillar and waited for the two drones to meet up.

Their creepy metal heads rotated full circle to get a good look at the entire intersection before heading their own ways to repeat their routes.

Then the scanned unit started heading back my direction.

I had a couple minutes before that steel jerk would be close enough for me to deactivate it and I always like to be thorough.

Lucky for me the fizzy drink machine I'd discovered was in the corner of the parking garage where I was hiding so I decided to do a little *shopping*.

Standing back but close enough for a deep scan I raised my hand and didn't have to wait more than a second to get the results...

Infected.

The power cord was cut and the buttons were all bashed in.

This was the best thing citizens could usually manage in order to deactivate an appliance if they thought it was infected.

Standing behind the machine I quickly removed the back outer plate.

I held my left hand near the main board ready and waiting as I activated my right glove for some mild current.

Just enough to crack the internal service lock to open it up and grab myself a can while avoiding a full boot which might wake the megavirus…

I heard a click and the door swung open.

Easy peasy.

I wasn't surprised to see that most of the cans were burst open but I had to hold in my excitement when I saw a couple childhood favorites of "Ultrasurge" intact.

I slipped one into my belt pack and carefully crept back toward the eastern edge of the parking structure where the Superdrone was still slowly returning.

Just a little more.

A few steps more…

It stopped.

I waited patiently as its head swiveled before it made an about-face.

When it took its first loud clanging step back down the road to meet up with its friend *that's* when I darted out.

With my right hand I retrieved the Ultrasurge from my belt. Bolting toward the back of the metal beast I readied my glove with a small charge to boost my throw before letting the can rip right into my target where it exploded into a death sentence of conductive fizzy syrup justice.

Like clockwork I instantly followed up with a fully charged electrofork from my left glove.

My personal light show short-circuited the Superdrone before it dropped like a stiff board face-first into the cracked pavement.

I ran over to its remains and knelt down for a deep scan…

Perfect. No communications post-attack and no alerts triggered.

I may be hearing strange voices but my abilities are still sharp.

With a wave of my hand the logs were downloaded to my HUD as three additional red markers popped up onto my map.

Four Superdrones left…

A couple were shown patrolling to the northeast. Jett would have no trouble dealing with those units but I wanted the others for myself.

The long office building across the road to the east looked like my next best move.

After trotting back to grab another Ultrasurge I crossed the street and cracked the lock of the building's entrance door while hoping to later find a conveniently placed rear exit to get the drop on the next Superdrone.

First I'd see what sort of goodies I might scrounge up.

My belt had plenty of empty compartments just begging to be filled with more toys… and employees themselves are always the weakest links in the chain of company security.

I only checked two cubicles before I found someone's login credentials written on a notepad on the side of their desk.

So typical.

Like most companies that place seriously needed to hold some seminars on the basics of security.

Access to the user's email account was effortlessly obtained then glancing at the office directory I quickly found their facilities department's employee roster.

Aaaand bingo.

Storage closet located. First floor. Room #1Q down the hall and around the corner.

I bypassed the entry pad and a happy little treasure trove of options presented itself…

Utilizing high voltage battery packs along with heavy gauge wire and other components I was able to assemble three powerful stun cells that would activate a nasty arc upon impact.

An assortment of flammable liquids and chemicals made fashioning some mini flame vials and makeshift firecrackers a cinch.

I crafted a couple of each and my belt pack now carried a little more insurance to deal with the metal morons outside.

The Rebellion would never condone unnecessary destruction of property... but a little noise pollution in the middle of the street would be a sweet distraction if I needed it.

I found the rear emergency exit as anticipated and it was ideal.

Peering out the tinted office windows I caught sight of the closest Superdrone. It was on its way back to the intersection right outside.

And I was especially eager to test out one of my stun cells.

After deactivating the exit alarm and charging one of my gloves *just in case...* I slowly opened the door as the stupid robot continued its march southbound past the eastern wall of the office building.

Grabbing a cell from my belt I hurled it right at its back and listened to the sweet serenade of sizzling microchips.

Witnessing the convulsing steel was a satisfying spectacle and before long there was nothing left but a stationary clump of shimmering scrap.

I savored the event with a grin plastered on my face.

ImperiCorp can get screwed.

I took a moment to psyche myself up knowing the next intersection might not be so smooth... because the scanned vehicles were right around the corner.

The automobiles *were* both sincerely abandoned and totally depleted of any charge they once held.

The megavirus is resilient but just like any software it still requires powered hardware to actively function.

Sadly... as soon as I caught a view of those cars my nerves took a frazzling that ended up costing me.

I started seeing images in my head from a heartbreaking tale I'd heard from Lorik.

Shortly before I was recruited to The Rebellion he'd lost a good friend to the wrath of an infected vehicle's front bumper and that's all I could think about as I scanned each one.

When the second car came up clean... my hands were shaking and I was in a cold sweat.

A totally hypnotic stupor.

I could still hear every syllable of Lorik's voice lamenting the loss of his fellow rebel.

He was a hard character tough as nails on the surface. But the day he told that story I could see that little piece of him that was broken forever.

It terrified me.

During my flashback I'd let down my guard and one of the nearby patrolling Superdrones targeted me.

I hadn't even *heard* its metal clangs as it approached since I was trapped in that mesmerized state...

A moderate phaser blast to my left arm did a good job of snapping me out of it. I was knocked flat on my back and the entire left side of my upper body was numb from the impact.

Quickly clinching and releasing my right hand I let loose a wide electrofork toward the drone as best I could.

The paltry charge combined with my clumsy aim was only enough to lightly stun it.

Fortunately that's all I needed.

While that rusty bozo was busy spasming to figure out what happened I grabbed the other Ultrasurge from my belt.

Lying there on the ground in my anxious panic I'd forgotten to charge my throw. With my weakened state producing a flabby toss the can bounced off the stupid cyborg's torso onto the ground and rolled away.

It boiled my blood.

Thank goodness I still carried two stun cells.

Flinging one hard and hitting my target... the innards of the Superdrone caught fire and sparks flew out from its body which granted me no small amount of personal gratification.

It was thorough but far from a quick and clean kill.

The other downside is that the impact from the overload was wide enough to burst open my Ultrasurge on the street.

Good gravy. I could have kept it for later!

I can't stand wasting resources but the important thing is that I'm still here... and telling from the lack of enemy markers on my HUD it looks like Jett has worked his craft and then some.

I've completed scanning the log from the fried Superdrone and just as I feared it indicated having sent a message to ImperiCorp Headquarters of my presence *and* location.

I'm going to dread telling Jett...

We've got to move.

Fast.

14

IMPERICORP HQ MASTER LOG
5/13 6:49 p.m.

Forces down in several blocks.

Superdrone units #G13 and #G23 have failed to return status queries. Class II unit #J42 directed to their patrol routes to investigate.

Partial remains of units located, both missing cranial modules. Plasma blade evidence on upper torsos.

Superdrone unit #G88 identified and engaged additional Runner near southwestern border of Central Zone. Deactivated by circuit overload.

Multiple Runners confirmed.

Threat level: High.

All drones notified.

15

JETT'S LOG
5/13 7:03 p.m.

An unexpected development: I am sitting in a small, abandoned power station next to none other than my fellow Runner, Nerva.

Not only was she called during my active run — she had been transported to my location upon passing through her first Glimmer Ring.

Despite our teamwork having been proven most efficient, the mysterious nature of The Fates grows exponentially.

I will soon elaborate.

My muscles are tired, yet my morale stands high. The sour mood I had nursed from the rough jaunt within the sewers has nearly disappeared, and I now carry a newfound level of confidence.

After Nerva joined me in the field, we split up and settled on a middle rendezvous point between us and the next Glimmer Ring.

I kept my distance, making sure to not stray too far to leave her without backup — in case she needed it.

She did not.

As she approached our selected checkpoint, a smile graced her lips as she jived, "Picking on more Superdrones I see? And you said *I* was seeking glory?"

I grinned while returning my plasma blade to my pack. "I can honestly say they — lost their heads over me."

I blinked long as I finished, "It was unavoidable, the block further north was too risky," and that was a lie.

I had been worried about her, yet I realized it would be an insult to her intelligence had I confessed I was helping to keep her safe.

The reality was that I never needed to.

I had the great pleasure of catching the intimidating sight of her melting down a Superdrone earlier tonight as I crouched under an awning from afar.

Nerva is clearly one Runner the drones ought not to tangle with, and her aptitude is bar none.

I continued to hold my own as well, having maintained complete stealth since my last entry.

Obtaining proper intel works wonders for one's performance, and I adjusted my tactics to better avoid the silent Class IIs.

Their communication system is far more sophisticated than the standard Phaserdrones, perhaps fast enough to send damage reports to ImperiCorp even when cleanly dispatched by a plasma blade.

Because of this, I opted to evade them rather than engage — in order to avoid drawing further attention. The closer we get to ImperiCorp Headquarters, the more crucial it is to remain undetected if we intend to take down their mainframe tonight.

Heavy turrets have an impressive range, and they are a force to be taken seriously.

Since deactivating the Superdrones closest to Nerva (about which I am admittedly ashamed), I have favored an elevated path.

The Class IIs had shown mainly to patrol the ground level just like their inferior counterparts. Nevertheless, now that Nerva and I had reunited, we were officially within range of ImperiCorp's mounted turrets.

Trusting we make it to the next ring, we will have properly flying surveillance drones to deal with as well.

I pray a fantastic journey into another putrid and *more active* sewer system does not find its way onto my itinerary. Had I foreseen such a possibility, I would have considered procuring an oxygen mask from the safe house.

I digress.

Though I had been fortunate enough to not take further damage, Nerva suffered a substantial phaser blast at close range, putting her Panicsuit level at 70%.

After reuniting at the street corner below, Nerva defeated the closest entry lock of the building, as she thought it best we snoop around inside for another advantage.

As usual, she was right.

An unsecured terminal was well utilized, and with little effort Nerva made use of a code fragment she had found within the downloaded log of a Superdrone to hack into the ImperiCorp surveillance system, and upload all ground threat locations to our HUDs.

Also obtained were the coordinates of the flying units, so we could now see their every move.

Although this was managed undetected while in the act, Nerva felt it necessary to clarify a lingering risk:

"As far as I can tell they aren't running any active scripts that can track my activity. But if an ImperiCorp employee sends the right query they'll see that the ID number of a deactivated Superdrone was used to log on to their system. I can't say when that'll happen. We're at the mercy of how active their staff is... and it won't take them long to put the pieces together once they run that report."

She continued with a shaky voice:

"Especially since they ID'd me *and* my location down the block."

"Then we should both maintain a low profile for the time being."

She nodded in agreement, and we continued to the rooftops.

This brings me back to my mention of The Fates.

As transmissions with active Runners are heavily discouraged, I was alarmed by a communication I received from Rebel Headquarters when we reached the rooftop, or so I *thought* it was them — for a split second.

A voice called out. It was not from any rebel.

"take...quarter..."

Nerva and I had been pacing, breathing slow and deep to settle our nerves atop the building. When I heard those words, I stopped dead in my tracks.

Looking behind me, I realized that she had, too.

For the first time as long as I could remember, she saw right through me. I wore the same gawking stare that she did, and our eyes were both locked in awe.

"Jett! Oh my gosh... you heard that too. You *finally heard them* didn't you?!"

"Heard *who?* Nerva, who *is* that?"

"...last time...an help you...while"

Another message — and as our eyes widened like those of feral cats on high alert, I knew we again both heard it simultaneously.

"It's the Fates. I *know* it's The Fates."

"That cannot be, Nerva. If it was not through our comms, then what you suggest implies either telepathy or hallucinations."

"Hallucinations? Really? The *same voice* in our heads caused by hallucinations? They're reaching out to us! I have no clue how but I know you heard them too and they're trying to help!"

"Take quarter?" I repeated it out loud, then twice more, still in half-disbelief.

"Yes. Take quarter! And it's that same confident voice. It spoke to me earlier telling me they knew I had what it takes... that *we* have what it takes. To defeat ImperiCorp. Another voice called out for help in my bunk today and now they're trying to help *us* here in the field."

The words leaving her lips were those of madness, yet her demeanor was as sure and sane as one could ask for.

"...take...quarter."

There it was again.

Our eyes widened, slightly lesser this time.

"Nerva, are they to be *trusted?* They could be just as vulnerable as us, or even ImperiCorp themselves hacking our comms."

"We can trust them. You've got to trust *me* on this. Okay?"

After a moment of contemplation, I nodded.

She scanned the area, and on the corner of the rooftop was a small empty facility room revealed to be a former power station — the same one we now sit in.

Taking quarter as we were advised by our assumed allies.

Before long, I broke the uneasy stillness within the musty old space.

"How long have you been hearing the voices?"

She replied, more calmly now. "A few days ago I heard one for the first time. It was a deeper voice than this one but too faint to make out. The transmission… if that's what we can call it… was unclear. Today I've heard more. Both from female voices."

I continued to breathe, trying to accept this new reality. "How long are we to shelter in place?"

"No idea… I don't know if they'll contact us again or if we should use our own judgment?"

We both nodded slowly, welcoming more silence which was now a comfort.

Comfort that did not last, as four blinking dots appeared on our HUD, moving at a pace neither of us had seen before, not by any class of drone — two by two, heading west from the direction of the skyscraper.

They were flying drones traveling at rooftop elevation, approaching our building with unsettling speed. We could only assume they were upgrades — more unexpected upgrades.

Nerva pressed a finger against the back of her right glove and whispered, "They're scanning the buildings actively with infrared. We need to stay very still."

Both of us complied.

Fortunately, the thick concrete walls of this old power station serve as an excellent barrier, as all four units continued past the building as they chirped rhythmically.

It would be a dishonest statement if I said our hearts were not pounding; we took to sitting down to collect our wits after the scare.

When a full minute elapsed after the flying drones had gone, Nerva began to speak — venting to help calm herself further.

"I hate them… I hate them *all*."

"As do I. We all do."

She stared past me into space and continued with intense, profound inflection, "People never learn… do they…"

"In what manner?"

"Jett… did you ever read the full primer on ImperiCorp's history?"

I had been obsessed with my physical training since joining The Rebellion.

I shook my head. "Not completely, no."

"They weren't always called ImperiCorp. They were just another tech manufacturer at first. Innocent as the rest trying to make a buck with the next best thing."

"Nerva, that is business. That is what companies do."

She continued, still staring into nowhere:

"...Then they grew and swallowed up company after company. Manipulating society with one tiny lifestyle change after another until citizens became so entitled and reliant on technology to maintain their simple little lives. They never even stopped to just *question* whether the changes were sound."

"Or without risk," I replied, understanding her gist. "Did our intel reveal exactly how they started?"

"We know they got the upper hand with the subtle consistent breakdown of privacy. The more tech that was released... the lazier society became. The company's biggest breakthrough was said to have been marketed as a device 'promising marvelous leaps in the business world, and newfound convenience to everyday life.'"

I failed to abstain from scoffing. "As generic and canned a tagline as any. What was the product?"

"We don't know. It was such a long time ago and volumes of documentation about the company's history have been methodically destroyed by the megavirus... especially the details about their transformation into the invasive monster as they're known today. But Jett the people just *let it happen*. They gave away all their freedoms… bit by bit."

It was unclear whether or not her pun was intended.

"Quite literally, it seems," I responded. "Yet those details are not relevant at this moment. What *is* — will be the final detonation of our pulse orbs before the end of tonight."

I offered Nerva the clearest wink and a nod, accompanied by my most sincere smile.

She took a moment to breathe before finally nodding back, her manner once again sharp and driven.

"Right… Let's do this."

We both made eye contact, and Nerva nodded once more as she cracked open the door, carefully stepped outside, then scanned our surroundings.

With a temperate smile, she returned to the shelter as her HUD readout synchronized with mine.

"Look… there's not a single drone in the sky and the closest heavy turret to the east is pointed away from us. I think now's our big chance to cross over into the Central Zone."

As we looked around within the walls of our hiding place, the same voice from before reached out to us both:

"ok… go."

"That's our queue… *do you trust them now?*"

I did indeed.

Our plan is to stay elevated as long as possible until the next Glimmer Ring — it waits upon the second floor of a commercial building two more blocks away, and we will then have a major hurdle to deal with:

That heavy turret.

Nerva is confident she can find a terminal in one of the lower floors of the building where it sits, to hack in and commandeer it for later use.

Though it is not within range to fire an accurate shot at the skyscraper, it will profoundly draw attention away from us when we are ready to slip into ImperiCorp Headquarters.

She is opening the door to perform one more scan, and if the area is truly clear we will begin ou###

-LOG CORRUPTED-

16

LORIK'S LOG
5/13 7:03 p.m.

    Somethin's not right.

    First Nerva gets called alongside Jett, they make it further than any Runner in weeks, and outta nowhere Jett's marker drops off my HUD.

    What 'appened?

    I don't like this one bit. If he was heavily attacked, he should'a ended up back here in his bunk. I'm not hearin' any transporters.

    That's a raw deal The Fates called Nerva to join in the fight while leaving me here stewin' in my bunk to worry about the two of'm.

    Hey wait. Nerva's marker's not movin'.

    Is ImperiCorp scramblin' our system or someth###

-LOG CORRUPTED-

17

NERVA'S LOG
5/13 7:03 p.m.

    I don't know what's wrong with him but Jett is seriously not okay.
    Not breathing. Not blinking. Not moving.
    I've scanned his vitals and he's otherwise fine but...
    He's completely paralyzed.
    ...It's getting worse whatever this is. I held a finger to his neck right now and I can't feel a pulse anymore... he just sits upright and totally rigid here on the fl###

-LOG CORRUPTED-

18

May 13, 1983 7:03 p.m.

"Nooo! Why is it *doing* this?

"Oh, not now, that's the furthest we've made it. *This is so lame!"*

A soft and kind voice whimpered, "Audrey, is it broken again?

"Yah, it looks like it's frozen up. I'll tell the counter. Go over to Mom and Dad, alright? I'll be right there. Don't worry, I'm sure they'll give us our money back again."

"*Oh*-kaaaay."

With short sulking steps across the floor of the dimly lit pizza parlor, the well-mannered young girl returned to the dark round wooden table where her father was shaking excessive amounts of Parmesan cheese onto his third slice of pepperoni.

His wife chuckled while asking, "You want some pizza with your cheese, babe?"

Her husband replied while chewing a mouthful, "Could've used a little more Parmesan," holding back laughter with white dust coating his lips.

Naomi crawled onto the wooden bench to greet her parents.

"Daddy, the game's broken again."

"Oh no! The same one as before?"

She replied with a whine, "Yaaaaah."

"Did your sister let you play too, this time?"

"Yes Mommy she did a lot! I had to ask for her help right away but she told me how to beat some bad guys and then she played with me at the same time! Then the next levels were really really hard and she even told me to take her last quarter to help me just in case but I didn't need it because right when she said to go to the next place it broke before we even got a Game Over!"

Their mother was flabbergasted. "You two have been playing almost *an hour* on one quarter each?"

"Heh — there's no *way* that thing's not set on easy mode."

Naomi was doing her best to hold back her tears. "No Daddy it was really hard! We had to work together, and Audrey had, another plan what to do next, and then, she said okay, lets go to the next building, and then, our players stuck and we couldn't move and now it's broken again!"

Audrey returned to the table with an older teenager following close behind to apologize.

"I'm sorry kids, here's your quarters back."

"Thank you mister," said Naomi, taking the coins in her tiny hands with a sniffle. "Is the game fixed yet?"

"Naaaw I'm sorry, it's gonna be out of order the rest of the night. It looks like I'll have to call our game vendor, and he'll fix it right up for next time. Sorry again, folks."

"No problem, we have to be going soon, anyway. Could we get a box for rest of this?"

"Sure thing, sir."

"Awww do we have to go, Mommy?"

"Yes, but don't worry, we'll be back soon, I promise."

Naomi's older sister cheered her up as she spoke with care and confidence, "Yah don't worry, next time when it's fixed, we'll play it again, get even further, beat ImperiCorp and win the game! Does that sound good?"

Her sister perked up with a smile.

"Yaaaah and next time *I* want to be Nerva!"

"Haha, okay. I think I'll try playing with Lorik. It says he runs the fastest."

"Okay, off to the car. Homeward bound!" their mother announced as she grabbed a pizza box. "Audrey, can you take your sister?"

"Sure, Mom."

Naomi reluctantly grasped her older sister's outstretched palm, turning one last time to catch a glimpse back at the arcade game in the far corner.

She saw the same older teenager walk up to it and tape an "OUT OF ORDER" sign to the middle of the screen, and as he unplugged the machine Naomi watched sadly as the colorfully backlit title at the top of the cabinet for "Runner Available" faded slowly to black.

Her mother stood up from the bench. "Can you grab the other pizza, babe?"

The father didn't answer. His eyes were glued to a TV above the nearby bar.

"Hey honey, look at this. Can you believe it? Like they'll *ever* sell these things... they're almost the price of a *car!*"

His wife turned her head to catch the tail end of the advertisement:

"...world's first commercially available cellular telephone can now be yours to own. A revolution promising marvelous leaps in the business world, and newfound convenience to everyday life..."

ABOUT THE AUTHOR

Michael is a computer geek/band geek hybrid from Generation X, raised in the quaint Danish village of Solvang, California. He has enjoyed a fruitful career in the computer and tech support industries for over 25 years.

Outside the cubicle, he can be found recording music in his home studio, brewing ale & mead, hosting board game parties, as well as playing plenty of video games with powerfully moving soundtracks.

Always one to enjoy thought-provoking tales of science fiction, he's at last fulfilled his desire to raise the eyebrows of fellow geeks.

He still misses Saturday morning cartoons and music videos, dearly.

Other books by Michael Anthony White:

TRUE TALES FROM THE LAND OF DIGITAL SAND

*ESSENTIAL INFORMATION AFTER
HIGH SCHOOL GRADUATION*

NEVER CRAVEN WAS THE RAVEN

Available at www.voxgeekus.com

ABOUT THE BOOK

Originally released as an eBook under the pen name of Matt Brewer, this book was written by Michael Anthony White as part of the 2024 Inkfort Press Publishing Derby.

*You can view the other books
published during the 2024 Derby below:*

https://www.inkfortpress.com/derby/2024

ACKNOWLEDGMENTS

My Wife, Kelly: For always being there for me with love and support throughout life, this entire project of passion, and beyond.

My Family: For love and support, always.

Felicia Day, Sandeep Parikh, Chris Pirillo, and Wil Wheaton: For motivating, encouraging, and sticking up for geeks around the world.